# RABBIT

Tonight's the night:
Rabbit Bright *will* turn
off the **light**.

"But wait,
where does the **light**
go when it's **dark?**"

To my mummy and daddy, thank you for believing in me
and giving me the freedom to explore the world

HODDER CHILDREN'S BOOKS
First published in Great Britain in 2020 by Hodder and Stoughton.

Text and illustrations copyright © Viola Wang, 2020

A CIP catalogue record for this book is available from the British Library.

HB ISBN: 978 1 444 94891 2
PB ISBN: 978 1 444 94892 9

1 3 5 7 9 10 8 6 4 2

Printed and bound in China

FSC
www.fsc.org

MIX
Paper from
responsible sources
FSC® C104740

Hodder Children's Books, an imprint of Hachette Children's Group, part of Hodder and Stoughton
Carmelite House, 50 Victoria Embankment, London, EC4Y 0DZ

An Hachette UK Company
www.hachette.co.uk
www.hachettechildrens.co.uk

Rabbit Bright sets out
into the blue-black night.
"If there's dark,
there must be light."

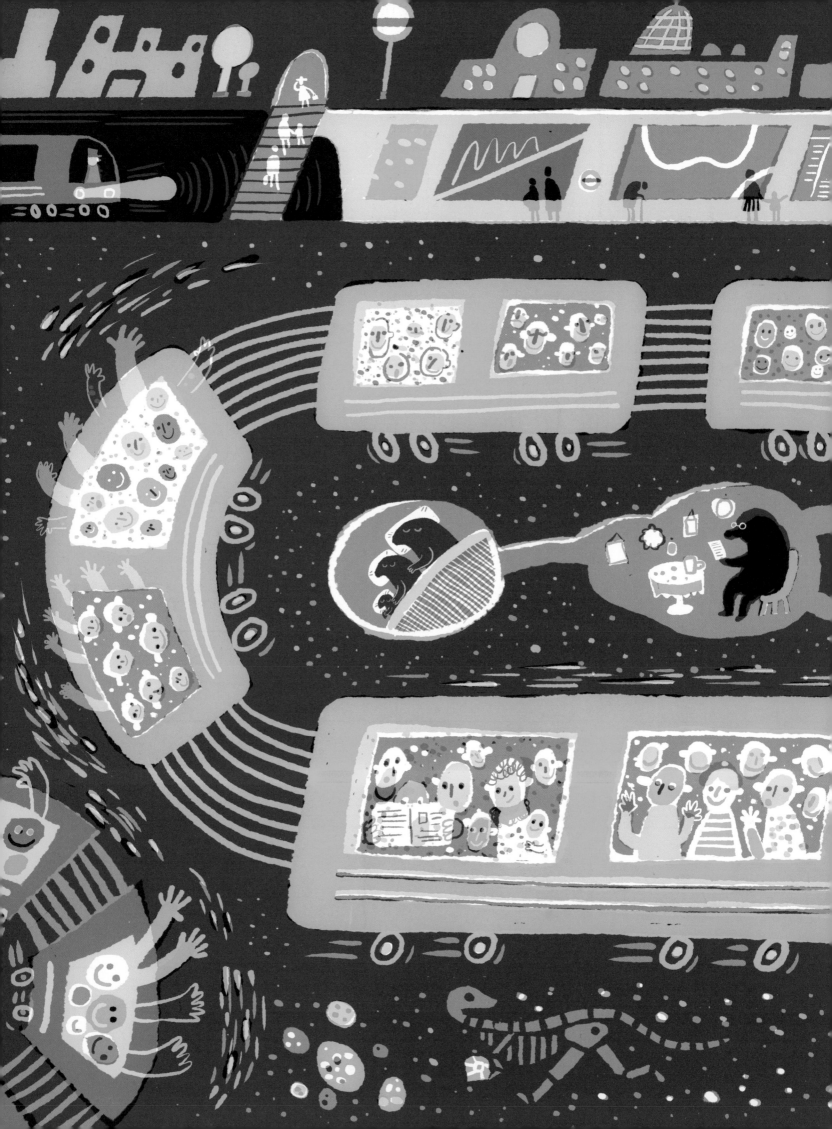

"And listen!" The underground train rumbles deep below the city. It glows in the tunnels, bringing everyone safely home.

"Now hush!"
The forest is dense and still.
Shy creatures of the night
light the way with their
bright eyes.

Flutter, flutter, flutter,
in the heart of a cave
as dark as a
bat's wing.

Little fireflies float and flash in the air.

Down,
down, down,
to the bottom of the sea.
It's as black as squid's ink.
"Has light ever reached
this deep?"

**Oh yes, it has!**
Wonderful creatures, **big** and small,
shine **bright** wherever they go.

Up, up, **up**,
to the top of the hill,
where the sky is velvet blue.
Still the **moon** smiles down,
and millions of stars
**twinkle and shimmer.**

"And beyond the stars?
Is there **light** at the end
of the universe?"

There will always
be **light** for those
who seek it.

But now a
warm bed is calling.
Good night, Rabbit Bright.

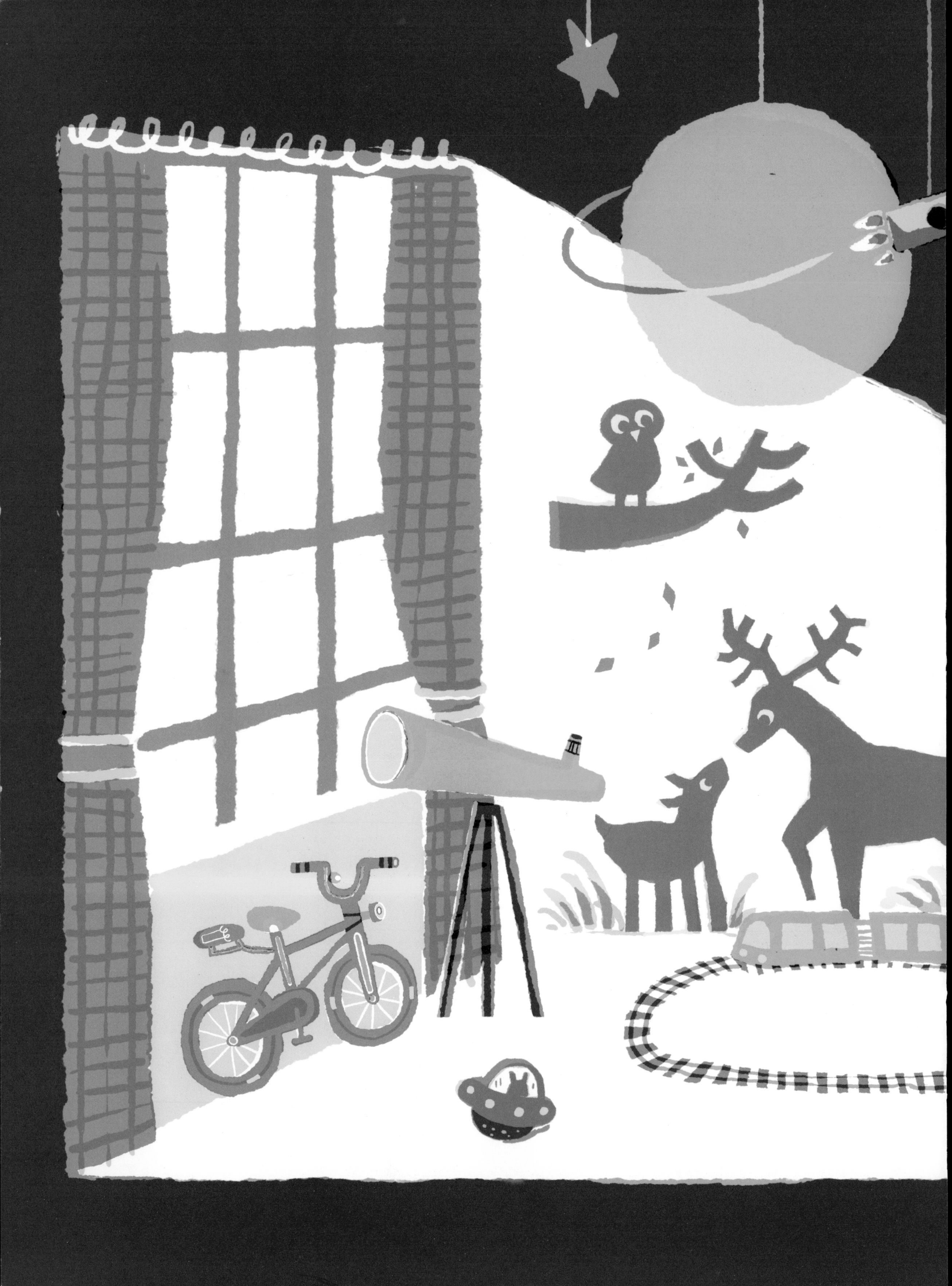